The Christmas Kalends of Provence

By

Thomas A. Janvier

The Christmas Kalends
of Provence

I

Fancy you've journeyed down the Rhône,
    Fancy you've passed Vienne, Valence,
Fancy you've skirted Avignon—
    And so are come *en pleine* Provence.

Fancy a mistral cutting keen
    Across the sunlit wintry fields,
Fancy brown vines, and olives green,
    And blustered, swaying, cypress shields.

Fancy a widely opened door,
    Fancy an eager outstretched hand,
Fancy—nor need you ask for more—
    A heart-sped welcome to our land.

Fancy the peal of Christmas chimes,
    Fancy that some long-buried year
Is born again of ancient times—
    And in Provence take Christmas cheer!

In my own case, this journey and this welcome were not fancies but realities. I had come to keep Christmas with my old friend Monsieur de Vièlmur according to the traditional Provençal rites and ceremonies in his own entirely Provençal home: an ancient dwelling which stands high up on the westward slope of the Alpilles, overlooking Arles and Tarascon and within sight of Avignon, near the Rhône margin of Provence.

The Vidame—such is Monsieur de Vièlmur's ancient title: dating from the vigorous days when every proper bishop, himself not averse to taking a breather with sword and battle-axe should fighting matters become serious, had his *vice dominus* to lead his forces in the field—is an old-school country gentleman who is amiably at odds with modern times. While tolerant of those who have yielded to the new order, he himself is a great stickler for the preservation of antique forms and ceremonies: sometimes, indeed, pushing his fancies to lengths that fairly would lay him open to the charge of whimsicality, were not even the most extravagant of his crotchets touched and mellowed by his natural goodness of heart. In the earlier stages of our acquaintance I was disposed to regard him as an eccentric; but a wider knowledge of Provençal matters has convinced me that he is a type. Under his genial guidance it has been my privilege to see much of the inner life of the Provençaux, and his explanations have enabled me to understand what I have seen: the Vidame being of an antiquarian and bookish temper, and never better pleased than when I set him to rummaging in his memory or his library for the information which I require to make clear to me some curious phase of Provençal manners or ways.

The Château de Vièlmur has remained so intimately a part of the Middle Ages that the subtle essence of that romantic period still pervades it, and gives to all that goes on there a quaintly archaic tone. The donjon, a prodigiously strong square tower dating from the twelfth century, partly is surrounded by a dwelling in the florid style of two hundred years back—the architectural flippancies of which have been so tousled by time and weather as to give it the look of an old beau caught unawares by age and grizzled in the midst of his affected youth.

In the rear of these oddly coupled structures is a farm-house with a dependent rambling collection of farm-buildings; the whole enclosing a large open court to which access is had by a vaulted passage-way, that on occasion may be closed by a double set of ancient iron-clamped doors. As the few exterior windows of the farm-house are grated heavily, and as from each of the rear corners of the square there projects a crusty tourelle from which a raking fire could be kept up along the walls, the place has quite the air of a testy little fortress—and a fortress it was meant to be when it was built three hundred years and more ago (the date, 1561, is carved on the keystone of the arched entrance) in the time of the religious wars.

But now the iron-clamped doors stand open on rusty hinges, and the court-yard has that look of placid cheerfulness which goes with the varied peaceful activities of farm labour and farm life. Chickens and ducks wander about it chattering complacently, an aged goat of a melancholy humour stands usually in one corner lost in misanthropic thought, and a great flock of extraordinarily tame pigeons flutters back and forth between the stone dove-cote rising in a square tower above the farm-house and the farm well.

AT THE WELL

This well—enclosed in a stone well-house surmounted by a very ancient crucifix—is in the centre of the court-yard, and it also is the centre of a little domestic world. To its kerb come the farm animals three times daily; while as frequently, though less regularly, most of the members of the two households come there too; and there do the humans—notably, I have observed, if they be of different sexes—find it convenient to rest for a while together and take a dish of friendly talk. From the low-toned chattering and the soft laughter that I have heard now and then of an evening I have inferred that these nominally chance encounters are not confined wholly to the day.

By simple machinery (of which the motive-power is an aged patient horse, who is started and left then to his own devices; and who works quite honestly, save that now and then he stops in his round and indulges himself in a little doze) the well-water is raised continuously into a long stone trough. Thence the overflow is led away to irrigate the garden of the Château: an old-fashioned garden, on a slope declining southward and westward, abounding in balustraded terraces and stone benches stiffly ornate, and having here and there stone nymphs and goddesses over which in summer climbing roses kindly (and discreetly) throw a blushing veil.

The dependent estate is a large one: lying partly on the flanks of the Alpilles, and extending far outward from the base of the range over the level region where the Rhône valley widens and merges into the valley of the Durance. On its highest slopes are straggling rows of almond trees, which in the early spring time belt the grey mountains with a broad girdle of delicate pink blossoms; a little lower are terraced olive-orchards, a pale shimmering green the year round—the olive continuously casting and renewing its leaves; and the lowest level, the wide fertile plain, is given over to vineyards and wheat-fields and fields of vegetables (grown for the Paris market), broken by plantations of fruit-trees and by the long lines of green-black cypress which run due east and west across the landscape and shield the tender growing things from the north wind, the mistral.

The Château stands, as I have said, well up on the mountain-side; and on the very spot (I must observe that I am here quoting its owner) where was the camp in which Marius lay with his legions until the time was ripe for him to strike the blow that secured Southern Gaul to Rome. This matter of Marius is a ticklish subject to touch on with the Vidame: since the fact must be admitted that other antiquaries are not less firm in their convictions, nor less hot in presenting them, that the camp of the Roman general was variously elsewhere—and all of them, I regret to add, display a lamentable acerbity of temper in scouting each other's views. Indeed, the subject is of so irritating a complexion that the mere mention of it almost surely will throw my old friend—who in matters not antiquarian has a sweetness of nature rarely equalled—into a veritable fuming rage.

But even the antiquaries are agreed that, long before the coming of the Romans, many earlier races successively made on this mountain promontory overlooking the Rhône delta their fortified home: for here, as on scores of other defensible heights throughout Provence, the merest scratching of the soil brings to light flints and potshards which tell of varied human occupancy in very far back times. And the antiquaries still farther are agreed that precisely as these material relics (only a little hidden beneath the present surface of the soil) tell of diverse ancient dwellers here, so do the surviving fragments of creeds and customs (only a little hidden beneath the surface of Provençal daily life) tell in a more sublimate fashion of those same vanished races which marched on into Eternity in the shadowy morning of Time.

For this is an old land, where many peoples have lived their spans out and gone onward—yet have not passed utterly away. Far down in the popular heart remnants of the beliefs and of the habits of those ancients survive, entranced: yet not so numbed but that, on occasion, they may be aroused into a life that still in part is real. Even now, when the touch-stone is applied—when the thrilling of some nerve of memory or of instinct brings the present into close association with the past—there will flash into view still quick particles of seemingly long-dead creeds or customs rooted in a deep antiquity: the faiths and usages which of old were cherished by the Kelto-Ligurians, Phœnicians, Grecians, Romans, Goths, Saracens, whose blood and whose beliefs are blended in the Christian race which inhabits Provence to-day.

II

In the dominion of Vièlmur there is an inner empire. Nominally, the Vidame is the reigning sovereign; but the power behind his throne is Misè Fougueiroun. The term "Misè" is an old-fashioned Provençal title of respect for women of the little bourgeoisie—tradesmen's and shopkeepers' wives and the like—that has become obsolescent since the Revolution and very generally has given place to the fine-ladyish "Madamo." With a little stretching, it may be rendered by our English old-fashioned title of "mistress"; and Misè Fougueiroun, who is the Vidame's housekeeper, is mistress over his household in a truly masterful way.

This personage is a little round woman, still plumply pleasing although she is rising sixty, who is arrayed always with an exquisite neatness in the dress—the sober black-and-white of the elder women, not the gay colours worn by the young girls—of the Pays d'Arles; and—although shortness and plumpness are at odds with majesty of deportment—she has, at least, the peremptory manner of one long accustomed to command. As is apt to be the way with little round women, her temper is of a brittle cast and her hasty rulings sometimes smack of injustice; but her nature (and this also is characteristic of her type) is so warmly generous that her heart easily can be caught into kindness on the rebound. The Vidame, who in spite of his antiquarian testiness is something of a philosopher, takes advantage of her peculiarities to compass such of his wishes as happen to run counter to her laws. His Machiavellian policy is to draw her fire by a demand of an extravagant nature; and then, when her lively refusal has set her a little in the wrong, handsomely to ask of her as a favour what he really requires—a method that never fails of success.

By my obviously sincere admiration of the Château and its surroundings, and by a discreet word or two implying a more personal admiration—a tribute which no woman of the Pays d'Arles ever is too old to accept graciously—I was so fortunate as to win Misè Fougueiroun's favour at the outset; a fact of which I was apprised on the evening of my arrival—it was at dinner, and the housekeeper herself had brought in a bottle of precious Châteauneuf-du-Pape—by the cordiality with which she joined forces with the Vidame in reprobating my belated coming to the Château. Actually, I was near a fortnight behind the time named in my invitation: which had stated expressly that Christmas began in Provence on the Feast of Saint Barbara, and that I was expected not later than that day—December 4th.

"Monsieur should have been here," said the housekeeper with decision, "when we planted the blessed Saint Barbara's grain. And now it is grown a full span. Monsieur will not see Christmas at all!"

But my apologetic explanation that I never even had heard of Saint Barbara's grain only made my case the more deplorable.

"Mai!" exclaimed Misè Fougueiroun, in the tone of one who faces suddenly a real calamity. "Can it be that there are no Christians in monsieur's

America? Is it possible that down there they do not keep the Christmas feast at all?"

To cover my confusion, the Vidame intervened with an explanation which made America appear in a light less heathenish. "The planting of Saint Barbara's grain," he said, "is a custom that I think is peculiar to the South of France. In almost every household in Provence, and over in Languedoc too, on Saint Barbara's day the women fill two, sometimes three, plates with wheat or lentils which they set afloat in water and then stand in the warm ashes of the fire-place or on a sunny window ledge to germinate. This is done in order to foretell the harvest of the coming year, for as Saint Barbara's grain grows well or ill so will the harvest of the coming year be good or bad; and also that there may be on the table when the Great Supper is served on Christmas Eve—that is to say, on the feast of the Winter Solstice—green growing grain in symbol or in earnest of the harvest of the new year that then begins.

PLANTING SAINT BARBARA'S GRAIN

"The association of the Trinitarian Saint Barbara with this custom," the Vidame continued, "I fear is a bit of a makeshift. Were three plates of grain the rule, something of a case would be made out in her favour. But the rule, so far as one can be found, is for only two. The custom must be of Pagan origin, and therefore dates from far back of the time when Saint Barbara lived in her three-windowed tower at Heliopolis. Probably her name was tagged to it because of old these votive and prophetic grain-fields were sown on what in Christian times became her dedicated day. But whatever light-mannered goddess may have been their patroness then, she is their patroness now; and from their sowing we date the beginning of our Christmas feast."

It was obvious that this explanation of the custom went much too far for Misè Fougueiroun. At the mention of its foundation in Paganism she sniffed audibly, and upon the Vidame's reference to the light-mannered goddess she drew her ample skirts primly about her and left the room.

The Vidame smiled. "I have scandalized Misè, and to-morrow I shall have to listen to a lecture," he said; and in a moment continued: "It is not easy to make our Provençaux realize how closely we are linked to older peoples and to older times. The very name for Christmas in Provençal, Calèndo, tells how this Christian festival lives on from the Roman festival of the Winter Solstice, the January Kalends; and the beliefs and customs which go with its celebration still more plainly mark its origin. Our farmers believe, for instance, that these days which now are passing—the twelve days, called *coumtié*, immediately preceding Christmas—are foretellers of the weather for the new twelve months to come; each in its turn, by rain or sunshine or by heat or cold, showing the character of the correspondingly numbered month of the new year. That the twelve prophetic days are those which immediately precede the solstice puts their endowment with prophetic power very far back into antiquity. Our farmers, too, have the saying, 'When Christmas falls on a Friday you may sow in ashes'—meaning that the harvest of the ensuing year surely will be so bountiful that seed sown anywhere will grow; and in this saying there is a strong trace of Venus worship, for Friday —Divèndre in Provençal—is the day sacred to the goddess of fertility and bears her name. That belief comes to us from the time when the statue of Aphrodite, dug up not long since at Marseille, was worshipped here. Our *Pater de Calèndo*—our curious Christmas prayer for abundance during the coming year—clearly is a Pagan supplication that in part has been diverted into Christian ways; and in like manner comes to us from Paganism the whole of our yule-log ceremonial."

The Vidame rose from the table. "Our coffee will be served in the library," he said. He spoke with a perceptible hesitation, and there was anxiety in his tone as he added: "Misè makes superb coffee; but sometimes, when I have offended her, it is not good at all." And he visibly fidgeted until the coffee arrived, and proved by its excellence that the housekeeper had been too noble to take revenge.

III

In the early morning a lively clatter rising from the farm-yard came through my open window, along with the sunshine and the crisp freshness of the morning air. My apartment was in the southeast angle of the Château, and my bedroom windows—overlooking the inner court—commanded the view along the range of the Alpilles to the Luberoun and Mont-Ventour, a pale great opal afloat in waves of clouds; while from the windows of my sitting-room I saw over Mont-Majour and Arles far across the level Camargue to the hazy horizon below which lay the Mediterrænean.

In the court-yard there was more than the ordinary morning commotion of farm life, and the buzz of talk going on at the well and the racing and shouting of a parcel of children all had in it a touch of eagerness and expectancy. While I still was drinking my coffee—in the excellence and delicate service of which I recognized the friendly hand of Misè Fougueiroun—there came a knock at my door; and, upon my answer, the Vidame entered—looking so elate and wearing so blithe an air that he easily might have been mistaken for a frolicsome middle-aged sunbeam.

"Hurry! Hurry!" he cried, while still shaking both my hands. "This is a day of days—we are going now to bring home the *cacho-fiò*, the yule-log! Put on a pair of heavy shoes—the walking is rough on the mountain-side. But be quick, and come down the moment that you are ready. Now I must be off. There is a world for me to do!" And the old gentleman bustled out of the room while he still was speaking, and in a few moments I heard him giving orders to some one with great animation on the terrace below.

When I went down stairs, five minutes later, I found him standing in the hall by the open doorway: through which I saw, bright in the morning light across the level landscape, King René's castle and the church of Sainte-Marthe in Tarascon; and over beyond Tarascon, high on the farther bank of the Rhône, Count Raymond's castle of Beaucaire; and in the far distance, faintly, the jagged peaks of the Cévennes.

But that was no time for looking at landscapes. "Come along!" he cried. "They all are waiting for us at the Mazet," and he hurried me down the steps to the terrace and so around to the rear of the Château, talking away eagerly as we walked.

"It is a most important matter," he said, "this bringing home of the *cacho-fiò*. The whole family must take part in it. The head of the family—the grandfather, the father, or the eldest son—must cut the tree; all the others must share in carrying home the log that is to make the Christmas fire. And the tree must be a fruit-bearing tree. With us it usually is an almond or an olive. The olive especially is sacred. Our people, getting their faith from their Greek ancestors, believe that lightning never strikes it. But an apple-tree or a pear-tree will serve the purpose, and up in the Alp region they burn the acorn-bearing oak. What we shall do to-day is an echo of Druidical ceremonial—of the time when the Druid priests cut the yule-oak and with their golden sickles reaped the sacred mistletoe; but old Jan here, who is so stiff for preserving ancient customs, does not know that this custom, like many others that he stands for, is the survival of a rite."

While the Vidame was speaking we had turned from the terrace and were nearing the Mazet—which diminutive of the Provençal word *mas*, meaning farm-house, is applied to the farm establishment at Vièlmur partly in friendliness and partly in indication of its dependence upon the great house, the Château. At the arched entrance we found the farm family awaiting us: Old Jan, the steward of the estate, and his wife Elizo; Marius, their elder son, a man over forty, who is the active manager of affairs; their younger son, Esperit, and their daughter Nanoun; and the wife of Marius, Janetoun, to whose skirts a small child was clinging while three or four larger children scampered about her in a whir of excitement over the imminent event by which Christmas really would be ushered in.

When my presentation had been accomplished—a matter a little complicated in the case of old Jan, who, in common with most of the old men hereabouts, speaks only Provençal—we set off across the home vineyard, and thence went upward through the olive-orchards, to the high region on the mountain-side where grew the almond-tree which the Vidame and his steward in counsel together had selected for the Christmas sacrifice.

Nanoun, a strapping red-cheeked black-haired bounce of twenty, ran back into the Mazet as we started; and joined us again, while we were crossing the vineyard, bringing with her a gentle-faced fair girl of her own age who came shyly. The Vidame, calling her Magali, had a cordial word for this new-comer; and nudged me to bid me mark how promptly Esperit was by her side. "It is as good as settled," he whispered. "They have been lovers since they were children. Magali is the daughter of Elizo's foster-sister, who died when the child was born. Then Elizo brought her home to the Mazet, and there she has lived her whole lifelong. Esperit is waiting only until he shall be established in the world to speak the word. And the scamp is in a hurry. Actually, he is pestering me to put him at the head of the Lower Farm!"

The Vidame gave this last piece of information in a tone of severity; but there was a twinkle in his kind old eyes as he spoke which led me to infer that Master Esperit's chances for the stewardship of the Lower Farm were anything but desperate, and I noticed that from time to time he cast very friendly glances toward these young lovers—as our little procession, mounting the successive terraces, went through the olive-orchards along the hill-side upward.

Presently we were grouped around the devoted almond-tree: a gnarled old personage, of a great age and girth, having that pathetic look of sorrowful dignity which I find always in superannuated trees—and now and then in humans of gentle natures who are conscious that their days of usefulness are gone. Esperit, who was beside me, felt called upon to explain that the old tree was almost past bearing and so was worthless. His explanation seemed to me a bit of needless cruelty; and I was glad when Magali, evidently moved by the same feeling, intervened softly with: "Hush, the poor tree may understand!" And then added, aloud: "The old almond must know that it is a very great honour for any tree to be chosen for the Christmas fire!"

This little touch of pure poetry charmed me. But I was not surprised by it—for pure poetry, both in thought and in expression, is found often among the peasants of Provence.

Even the children were quiet as old Jan took his place beside the tree, and there was a touch of solemnity in his manner as he swung his heavy axe and gave the first strong blow—that sent a shiver through all the branches, as though the tree realized that death had overtaken it at last. When he had slashed a dozen times into the trunk, making a deep gash in the pale red wood beneath the brown bark, he handed the axe to Marius; and stood watching silently with the rest of us while his son finished the work that he had begun. In a few minutes the tree tottered; and then fell with a growling death-cry, as its brittle old branches crashed upon the ground.

Whatever there had been of unconscious reverence in the silence that attended the felling was at an end. As the tree came down everybody shouted. Instantly the children were swarming all over it. In a moment our little company burst into the flood of loud and lively talk that is inseparable in Provence from gay occasions—and that is ill held in check even at funerals and in church. They are the merriest people in the world, the Provençaux.

IV

Marius completed his work by cutting through the trunk again, making a noble *cacho-fiò* near five feet long—big enough to burn, according to the Provençal rule, from Christmas Eve until the evening of New Year's Day.

It is not expected, of course, that the log shall burn continuously. Each night it is smothered in ashes and is not set a-blazing again until the following evening. But even when thus husbanded the log must be a big one to last the week out, and it is only in rich households that the rule can be observed. Persons of modest means are satisfied if they can keep burning the sacred fire over Christmas Day; and as to the very poor, their *cacho-fiò* is no more than a bit of a fruit-tree's branch—that barely, by cautious guarding, will burn until the midnight of Christmas Eve. Yet this suffices: and it seems to me that there is something very tenderly touching about these thin yule-twigs which make, with all the loving ceremonial and rejoicing that might go with a whole tree-trunk, the poor man's Christmas fire. In the country, the poorest man is sure of his *cacho-fiò*. The Provençaux are a kindly race, and the well-to-do farmers are not forgetful of their poorer neighbors at Christmas time. An almond-branch always may be had for the asking; and often, along with other friendly gifts toward the feast, without any asking at all. Indeed, as I understood from the Vidame's orders, the remainder of our old almond was to be cut up and distributed over the estate and about the neighborhood—and so the life went out from it finally in a Christmas blaze that brightened many homes. In the cities, of course, the case is different; and, no doubt, on many a chill hearth no yule-fire burns. But even in the cities this kindly usage is not unknown. Among the boat-builders and ship-wrights of the coast towns the custom long has obtained—being in force even in the Government dock-yard at Toulon—of permitting each workman to carry away a *cacho-fiò* from the refuse oak timber; and an equivalent present frequently is given at Christmas time to the labourers in other trades.

While the Vidame talked to me of these genial matters we were returning homeward, moving in a mildly triumphal procession that I felt to be a little tinctured with ceremonial practices come down from forgotten times. Old Jan and Marius marching in front, Esperit and the sturdy Nanoun marching behind, carried between them the yule-log slung to shoulder-poles. Immediately in their wake, as chief rejoicers, the Vidame and I walked arm in arm. Behind us came Elizo and Janetoun and Magali—save that the last (manifesting a most needless solicitude for Nanoun, who almost could have carried the log alone on her own strapping shoulders) managed to be frequently near Esperit's side. The children, waving olive-branches, careered about us; now and then going through the form of helping to carry the *cacho-fiò*, and all the while shouting and singing and dancing—after the fashion of small dryads who also were partly imps of joy. So we came down through the sun-swept, terraced olive-orchards in a spirit of rejoicing that had its beginning very far back in the world's history and yet was freshly new that day.

Our procession took on grand proportions, I should explain, because our yule-log was of extraordinary size. But always the yule-log is brought home in triumph. If it is small, it is carried on the shoulder of the father or the eldest son; if it is a goodly size, those two carry it together; or a young husband and wife may bear it between them—as we actually saw a thick branch of our almond borne away that afternoon—while the children caracole around them or lend little helping hands.

Being come to the Mazet, the log was stood on end in the court-yard in readiness to be taken thence to the fire-place on Christmas Eve. I fancied that the men handled it with a certain reverence; and the Vidame assured me that such actually was the case. Already, being dedicate to the Christmas rite, it had become in a way sacred; and along with its sanctity, according to the popular belief, it had acquired a power which enabled it sharply to resent anything that smacked of sacrilegious affront. The belief was well rooted, he added by way of instance, that any one who sat on a yule-log would pay in his person for his temerity either with a dreadful stomach-ache that would not permit him to eat his Christmas dinner, or would suffer a pest of boils. He confessed that he always had wished to test practically this superstition, but that his faith in it had been too strong to suffer him to make the trial!

On the other hand, when treated reverently and burned with fitting rites, the yule-log brings upon all the household a blessing; and when it has been consumed even its ashes are potent for good. Infused into a much-esteemed country-side medicine, the yule-log ashes add to its efficacy; sprinkled in the chicken-house and cow-stable, they ward off disease; and, being set in the linen-closet, they are an infallible protection against fire. Probably this last property has its genesis in the belief that live-coals from the yule-log may be placed on the linen cloth spread for the Great Supper without setting it on fire—a belief which prudent housewives always are shy of putting to a practical test.

The home-bringing ceremony being thus ended, we walked back to the Château together—startling Esperit and Magali standing hand in hand, lover-like, in the archway; and when we were come to the terrace, and were seated snugly in a sunny corner, the Vidame told me of a very stately yule-log gift that was made anciently in Aix—and very likely elsewhere also—in feudal times.

In Aix it was the custom, when the Counts of Provence still lived and ruled there, for the magistrates of the city each year at Christmas-tide to carry in solemn procession a huge *cacho-fiò* to the palace of their sovereign; and there formally to present to him—or, in his absence, to the Grand Seneschal on his behalf—this their free-will and good-will offering. And when the ceremony of presentation was ended the city fathers were served with a collation at the Count's charges, and were given the opportunity to pledge him loyally in his own good wine.

Knowing Aix well, I was able to fill in the outlines of the Vidame's bare statement of fact and also to give it a background. What a joy the procession must have been to see! The grey-bearded magistrates, in their velvet caps and robes, wearing their golden chains of office; the great log, swung to shoulder-poles and borne by leathern-jerkined henchmen; surely drummers and fifers, for such a ceremonial would have been impossibly incomplete in Provence without a *tambourin* and *galoubet*; doubtless a brace of ceremonial trumpeters; and a seemly guard in front and rear of steel-capped and steel-jacketed halbardiers. All these marching gallantly through the narrow, yet stately, Aix streets; with comfortable burghers and well-rounded matrons in the doorways looking on, and pretty faces peeping from upper windows and going all a-blushing because of the over-bold glances of the men-at-arms! And then fancy the presentation in the great hall of the castle; and the gay feasting; and the merry wagging of grey-bearded chins as the magistrates cried all together, "To the health of the Count!"—and tossed their wine!

I protest that I grew quite melancholy as I thought how delightful it all was —and how utterly impossible it all is in these our own dull times! In truth I never can dwell upon such genially picturesque doings of the past without feeling that Fate treated me very shabbily in not making me one of my own ancestors—and so setting me back in that hard-fighting, gay-going, and eminently light-opera age.

V

As Christmas Day drew near I observed that Misè Fougueiroun walked thoughtfully and seemed to be oppressed by heavy cares. When I met her on the stairs or about the passages her eyes had the far-off look of eyes prying into a portentous future; and when I spoke to her she recovered her wandering wits with a start. At first I feared that some grave misfortune had overtaken her; but I was reassured, upon applying myself to the Vidame, by finding that her seeming melancholy distraction was due solely to the concentration of all her faculties upon the preparation of the Christmas feast.

Her case, he added, was not singular. It was the same just then with all the housewives of the region: for the chief ceremonial event of Christmas in Provence is the *Gros Soupa* that is eaten upon Christmas Eve, and of even greater culinary importance is the dinner that is eaten upon Christmas Day—wherefore does every woman brood and labour that her achievement of those meals may realize her high ideal! Especially does the preparation of the Great Supper compel exhaustive thought. Being of a vigil, the supper necessarily is "lean"; and custom has fixed unalterably the principal dishes of which it must be composed. Thus limited straitly, the making of it becomes a struggle of genius against material conditions; and its successful accomplishment is comparable with the perfect presentment by a great poet of some well-worn elemental truth in a sonnet—of which the triumphant beauty comes less from the integral concept than from the exquisite felicity of expression that gives freshness to a hackneyed subject treated in accordance with severely constraining rules.

It is no wonder, therefore, that the Provençal housewives give the shortest of the December days to soulful creation in the kitchen, and the longest of the December nights to searching for inspired culinary guidance in dreams. They take such things very seriously, those good women: nor is their seriousness to be wondered at when we reflect that Saint Martha, of blessed memory, ended her days here in Provence; and that this notable saint, after delivering the country from the ravaging Tarasque, no doubt set up in her own house at Tarascon an ideal standard of housekeeping that still is in force. Certainly, the women of this region pattern themselves so closely upon their sainted model as to be even more cumbered with much serving than are womenkind elsewhere.

Because of the Vidame's desolate bachelorhood, the kindly custom long ago was established that he and all his household every year should eat their Great Supper with the farm family at the Mazet; an arrangement that did not work well until Misè Fougueiroun and Elizo (after some years of spirited squabbling) came to the agreement that the former should be permitted to prepare the delicate sweets served for dessert at that repast. Of these the most important is nougat, without which Christmas would be as barren in Provence as Christmas would be in England without plum-pudding or in

America without mince-pies. Besides being sold in great quantities by town confectioners, nougat is made in most country homes. Even the dwellers on the poor up-land farms—which, being above the reach of irrigation, yield uncertain harvests—have their own almond-trees and their own bees to make them honey, and so possess the raw materials of this necessary luxury. As for the other sweets, they may be anything that fancy and skill together can achieve; and it is in this ornate department of the Great Supper that genius has its largest chance.

But it was the making of the Christmas dinner that mainly occupied Misè Fougueiroun's mind—a feast pure and simple, governed by the one jolly law that it shall be the very best dinner of the whole year! What may be termed its by-laws are that the principal dish shall be a roast turkey, and that nougat and *poumpo* shall figure at the dessert. Why *poumpo* is held in high esteem by the Provençaux I am not prepared to say. It seemed to me a cake of only a humdrum quality; but even Misè Fougueiroun—to whom I am indebted for the appended recipe[1]—spoke of it in a sincerely admiring and chop-smacking way.

Anciently the Christmas bird was a goose—who was roasted and eaten ('twas a backhanded compliment!) in honour of her ancestral good deeds. For legend tells that when the Kings, led by the star, arrived at the inn-stable in Bethlehem it was the goose, alone of all the animals assembled there, who came forward politely to make them her compliments; yet failed to express clearly her good intentions because she had caught a cold, in the chill and windy weather, and her voice was unintelligibly creaky and harsh. The same voice ever since has remained to her, and as a farther commemoration of her hospitable and courteous conduct it became the custom to spit her piously on Christmas Day.

I have come across the record of another Christmas roast that now and then was served at the tables of the rich in Provence in mediæval times. This was a huge cock, stuffed with chicken-livers and sausage-meat and garnished with twelve roasted partridges, thirty eggs, and thirty truffles: the whole making an alimentary allegory in which the cock represented the year, the partridges the months, the eggs the days, and the truffles the nights. But this never was a common dish, and not until the turkey appeared was the goose rescued from her annual martyrdom.

The date of the coming of the turkey to Provence is uncertain. Popular tradition declares that the crusaders brought him home with them from the Indies! Certainly, he came a long while ago; probably very soon after Europe received him from America as a noble and perpetual Christmas present—and that occurred, I think, about thirty years after Columbus, with an admirable gastronomic perception, discovered his primitive home.

Ordinarily the Provençal Christmas turkey is roasted with a stuffing of chestnuts, or of sausage-meat and black olives: but the high cooks of Provence also roast him stuffed with truffles—making so superb a dish that Brillat-Savarin has singled it out for praise. Misè Fougueiroun's method, still more exquisite, was to make a stuffing of veal and fillet of pork (one-third of the former and two-thirds of the latter) minced and brayed in a mortar with a seasoning of salt and pepper and herbs, to which truffles cut in quarters were added with a lavish hand. For the basting she used a piece of salt-pork fat stuck on a long fork and set on fire. From this the flaming juice was dripped judiciously over the roast, with resulting little puffings of brown skin which permitted the savour of the salt to penetrate the flesh and so gave to it a delicious crispness and succulence. As to the flavour of a turkey thus cooked, no tongue can tell what any tongue blessed to taste of it may know! Of the minor dishes served at the Christmas dinner it is needless to speak. There is nothing ceremonial about them; nothing remarkable except their excellence and their profusion. Save that they are daintier, they are much the same as Christmas dishes in other lands.

While the preparation of all these things was forward, a veritable culinary tornado raged in the lower regions of the Château. Both Magali and the buxom Nanoun were summoned to serve under the housekeeper's banners, and I was told that they esteemed as a high privilege their opportunity thus to penetrate into the very arcana of high culinary art. The Vidame even said that Nanoun's matrimonial chances—already good, for the baggage had set half the lads of the country-side at loggerheads about her—would be decidedly bettered by this discipline under Misè Fougueiroun: whose name long has been one to conjure with in all the kitchens between Saint-Remy and the Rhône. For the Provençaux are famous trencher-men, and the way that leads through their gullets is not the longest way to their hearts.

VI

But in spite of their eager natural love for all good things eatable, the Provençaux also are poets; and, along with the cooking, another matter was in train that was wholly of a poetic cast. This was the making of the crèche: a representation with odd little figures and accessories of the personages and scene of the Nativity—the whole at once so naïve and so tender as to be possible only among a people blessed with rare sweetness and rare simplicity of soul.

The making of the crèche is especially the children's part of the festival—though the elders always take a most lively interest in it—and a couple of days before Christmas, as we were returning from one of our walks, we fell in with all the farm children coming homeward from the mountains laden with crèche-making material: mosses, lichens, laurel, and holly; this last of smaller growth than our holly, but bearing fine red berries, which in Provençal are called *li poumeto de Sant-Jan*—"the little apples of Saint John."

Our expedition had been one of the many that the Vidame took me upon in order that he might expound his geographical reasons for believing in his beloved Roman Camp; and this diversion enabled me to escape from Marius—I fear with a somewhat unseemly precipitation—by pressing him for information in regard to the matter which the children had in hand. As to openly checking the Vidame, when once he fairly is astride of his hobby, the case is hopeless. To cast a doubt upon even the least of his declarations touching the doings of the Roman General is the signal for a blaze of arguments down all his battle front; and I really do not like even to speculate upon what might happen were I to meet one of his major propositions with a flat denial! But an attack in flank, I find—the sudden posing of a question upon some minor antiquarian theme—usually can be counted upon, as in this instance, to draw him outside the Roman lines. Yet that he left them with a pained reluctance was so evident that I could not but feel some twinges of remorse—until my interest in what he told me made me forget my heartlessness in shunting to a side track the subject on which he so loves to talk.

In a way, the crèche takes in Provence the place of the Christmas-tree, of which Northern institution nothing is known here; but it is closer to the heart of Christmas than the tree, being touched with a little of the tender beauty of the event which it represents in so quaint a guise. Its invention is ascribed to Saint Francis of Assisi. The chronicle of his Order tells that this seraphic man, having first obtained the permission of the Holy See, represented the principal scenes of the Nativity in a stable; and that in the stable so transformed he celebrated mass and preached to the people. All this is wholly in keeping with the character of Saint Francis; and, certainly, the crèche had its origin in Italy in his period, and in the same conditions which formed his graciously fanciful soul. Its introduction into Provence is said to have been in the time of John XXII.—the second of the Avignon Popes, who came to the Pontificate in the year 1316—and by the Fathers of the Oratory of Marseille: from which centre it rapidly spread abroad through the land until it became a necessary feature of the Christmas festival both in churches and in homes.

Obviously, the crèche is an offshoot from the miracle plays and mysteries which had their beginning a full two centuries earlier. These also survive vigorously in Provence in the "Pastouralo": an acted representation of the Nativity that is given each year during the Christmas season by amateurs or professionals in every city and town, and in almost every village. Indeed, the Pastouralo is so large a subject, and so curious and so interesting, that I venture here only to allude to it. Nor has it, properly—although so intensely a part of the Provençal Christmas—a place in this paper, which especially deals with the Christmas of the home.

In the farm-houses, and in the dwellings of the middle-class, the crèche is placed always in the living-room, and so becomes an intimate part of the family life. On a table set in a corner is represented a rocky hill-side—dusted with flour to represent snow—rising in terraces tufted with moss and grass and little trees and broken by foot-paths and a winding road. This structure is very like a Provençal hill-side, but it is supposed to represent the rocky region around Bethlehem. At its base, on the left, embowered in laurel or in holly, is a wooden or pasteboard representation of the inn; and beside the inn is the stable: an open shed in which are grouped little figures representing the several personages of the Nativity. In the centre is the Christ-Child, either in a cradle or lying on a truss of straw; seated beside him is the Virgin; Saint Joseph stands near, holding in his hand the mystic lily; with their heads bent down over the Child are the ox and the ass—for those good animals helped with their breath through that cold night to keep him warm. In the foreground are the two *ravi*—a man and a woman in awed ecstasy, with upraised arms—and the adoring shepherds. To these are added on Epiphany the figures of the Magi—the Kings, as they are called always in French and in Provençal—with their train of attendants, and the camels on which they have brought their gifts. Angels (pendent from the farm-house ceiling) float in the air above the stable. Higher is the Star, from which a ray (a golden thread) descends to the Christ-Child's hand. Over all, in a glory of clouds, hangs the figure of Jehovah attended by a white dove.

These are the essentials of the crèche; and in the beginning, no doubt, these made the whole of it. But for nearly six centuries the delicate imagination of the Provençal poets and the cruder, but still poetic, fancy of the Provençal people have been enlarging upon the simple original: with the result that twoscore or more figures often are found in the crèche of to-day.

Either drawing from the quaintly beautiful mediæval legends of the birth and childhood of Jesus, or directly from their own quaintly simple souls, the poets from early times have been making Christmas songs—noëls, or nouvé as they are called in Provençal—in which new subordinate characters have been created in a spirit of frank realism, and these have materialized in new figures surrounding the crèche. At the same time the fancy of the people, working with a still more naïve directness along the lines of associated ideas, has been making the most curiously incongruous and anachronistic additions to the group.

To the first order belong such creations as the blind man, led by a child, coming to be healed of his blindness by the Infant's touch; or that of the young mother hurrying to offer her breast to the new-born (in accordance with the beautiful custom still in force in Provence) that its own mother may rest a little before she begins to suckle it; or that of the other mother bringing the cradle of which her own baby has been dispossessed, because of her compassion for the poor woman at the inn whose child is lying on a truss of straw.

But the popular additions, begotten of association of ideas, are far more numerous and also are far more curious. The hill-top, close under the floating figure of Jehovah, has been crowned with a wind-mill—because wind-mills abounded anciently on the hill-tops of Provence. To the mill, naturally, has been added a miller—who is riding down the road on an ass, with a sack of flour across his saddle-bow that he is carrying as a gift to the Holy Family. The adoring shepherds have been given flocks of sheep, and on the hill-side more shepherds and more sheep have been put for company. The sheep, in association with the ox and the ass, have brought in their train a whole troop of domestic animals—including geese and turkeys and chickens and a cock on the roof of the stable; and in the train of the camels has come the extraordinary addition of lions, bears, leopards, elephants, ostriches, and even crocodiles! The Provençaux being from of old mighty hunters (the tradition has found its classic embodiment in Tartarin), and hill-sides being appropriate to hunting, a figure of a fowler with a gun at his shoulder has been introduced; and as it is well, even in the case of a Provençal sportsman, to point a gun at a definite object, the fowler usually is so placed as to aim at the cock on the stable roof. He is a modern, yet not very recent addition, the fowler, as is shown by the fact that he carries a flint-lock fowling-piece. Drumming and fifing being absolute essentials to every sort of Provençal festivity, a conspicuous figure always is found playing on a *tambourin* and *galoubet*. Itinerant knife-grinders are an old institution here, and in some obscure way—possibly because of their thievish propensities—are associated intimately with the devil; and so there is either a knife-grinder simple, or a devil with a knife-grinder's wheel. Of old it was the custom for the women to carry distaffs and to spin out thread as they went to and from the fields or along the roads (just as the women nowadays knit as they walk), and therefore a spinning-woman always is of the company. Because child-stealing was not uncommon here formerly, and because gypsies still are plentiful, there are three gypsies lurking about the inn all ready to steal the Christ-Child away. As the inn-keeper naturally would come out to investigate the cause of the commotion in his stable-yard, he is found, with the others, lantern in hand. And, finally, there is a group of women bearing as gifts to the Christ-Child the essentials of the Christmas feast: codfish, chickens, carde, ropes of garlic, eggs, and the great Christmas cakes, *poumpo* and *fougasso*.

Many other figures may be, and often are, added to the group—of which one of the most delightful is the Turk who makes a solacing present of his pipe to Saint Joseph; but all of these which I have named have come to be now quite as necessary to a properly made crèche as are the few which are taken direct from the Bible narrative: and the congregation surely is one of the quaintest that ever poetry and simplicity together devised!

In Provençal the diminutive of saint is *santoun*; and it is as santouns that all the personages of the crèche—including the whole of the purely human and animal contingent, and even the knife-grinding devil—are known. They are of various sizes—the largest, used in churches, being from two to three feet high—and in quality of all degrees: ranging downward from real magnificence (such as may be seen in the seventeenth-century Neapolitan crèche in Room V. of the Musée de Cluny) to the rough little clay figures two or three inches high in common household use throughout Provence. These last, sold by thousands at Christmas time, are as crude as they well can be: pressed in rude moulds, dried (not baked), and painted with glaring colours, with a little gilding added in the case of Jehovah and the angels and the Kings.

For two centuries or more the making of clay santouns has been a notable industry in Marseille. It is largely a hereditary trade carried on by certain families inhabiting that ancient part of the city, the Quarter of Saint-Jean, which lies to the south of the Vieux Port. The figures sell for the merest trifle, the cheapest for one or two sous, yet the Santoun Fair—held annually in December in booths set up in the Cour-du-Chapitre and in the Allée-des-Capucins—is of a real commercial importance; and is also—what with the oddly whimsical nature of its merchandise, and the vast enjoyment of the children under parental or grand-parental convoy who are its patrons—the very gayest sight in that city of which gayety is the dominant characteristic the whole year round.

VII

Not until "the day of the Kings," the Feast of the Epiphany, is the crèche completed. Then are added to the group the figures of the three Kings—the Magi, as we call them in English: along with their gallant train of servitors, and the hump-backed camels on which they have ridden westward to Bethlehem guided by the Star. The Provençal children believe that they come at sunset, in pomp and splendour, riding in from the outer country, and on through the street of the village, and in through the church door, to do homage before the manger in the transept where the Christ-Child lies. And the children believe that it may be seen, this noble procession, if only they may have the good fortune to hit upon the road along which the royal progress to their village is to be made. But Mistral has told about all this far better than I can tell about it, and I shall quote here, by his permission, a page or two from the "Memoirs" which he is writing, slowly and lovingly, in the between-whiles of the making of his songs:

"To-morrow's the festival of the Kings. This evening they arrive. If you want to see them, little ones, go quickly to meet them—and take presents for them, and for their pages, and for the poor camels who have come so far!"

That was what, in my time, the mothers used to say on the eve of Epiphany —and, *zòu!* all the children of the village would be off together to meet "les Rois Mages," who were coming with their pages and their camels and the whole of their glittering royal suite to adore the Christ-Child in our church in Maillane! All of us together, little chaps with curly hair, pretty little girls, our sabots clacking, off we would go along the Arles road, our hearts thrilling with joy, our eyes full of visions. In our hands we would carry, as we had been bidden, our presents: fougasso for the Kings, figs for the pages, sweet hay for the tired camels who had come so far.

On we would go through the cold of dying day, the sun, over beyond the Rhône, dipping toward the Cévennes; leafless trees, red in low sun-rays; black lines of cypress; in the fields an old woman with a fagot on her head; beside the road an old man scratching under the hedge for snails.

"Where are you going, little ones?"

"We are going to meet the Kings!" And on we would run proudly along the white road, while the shrewd north wind blew sharp behind us, until our old church tower would drop away and be hidden behind the trees. We could see far, far down the wide straight road, but it would be bare! In the cold of the winter evening all would be dumb. Then we would meet a shepherd, wrapped in his long brown cloak and leaning on his staff, a silhouette against the western sky.

"Where are you going, little ones?"

"We are going to meet the Kings! Can you tell us if they are far off?"

"Ah, the Kings. Certainly. They are over there behind the cypresses. They are coming. You will see them soon."

On we would run to meet the Kings so near, with our fougasso and our figs and our hay for the hungry camels. The day would be waning rapidly, the sun dropping down into a great cloud-bank above the mountains, the wind nipping us more shrewdly as it grew still more chill. Our hearts also would be chilling. Even the bravest of us would be doubting a little this adventure upon which we were bound.

THE PASSING OF THE KINGS

Then, of a sudden, a flood of radiant glory would be about us, and from the dark cloud above the mountains would burst forth a splendour of glowing crimson and of royal purple and of glittering gold!

"Les Rois Mages! Les Rois Mages!" we would cry. "They are coming! They are here at last!"

But it would be only the last rich dazzle of the sunset. Presently it would vanish. The owls would be hooting. The chill night would be settling down upon us, out there in the bleak country, sorrowful, alone. Fear would take hold of us. To keep up our courage a little, we would nibble at the figs which we had hoped to give to the pages, at the fougasso which we had hoped to present to the Kings. As for the hay for the hungry camels, we would throw it away. Shivering in the wintry dusk, we would return sadly to our homes.

And when we reached our homes again our mothers would ask: "Well, did you see them, the Kings?"

"No; they passed by on the other side of the Rhône, behind the mountains."

"But what road did you take?"

"The road to Arles."

"Ah, my poor child! The Kings don't come that way. They come from the East. You should have gone out to meet them on the road to Saint-Remy. And what a sight you have missed! Oh, how beautiful it was when they came marching into Maillane—the drums, the trumpets, the pages, the camels! *Mon Dieu*, what a commotion! What a sight it was! And now they are in the church, making their homage before the manger in which the little Christ-Child lies. But never mind; after supper you shall see them all."

Then we would sup quickly, and so be off to the church, crowded with all Maillane. Barely would we be entered there when the organ would begin, at first softly and then bursting forth formidably, all our people singing with it, with the superb noël:

In the early morning
I met a train
Of three great Kings who were going on a journey!

High up before the altar, directly above the manger in which the Christ-Child was lying, would be the glittering *bello estello*; and making their homage before the manger would be the Kings whom it had guided thither from the East: old white-bearded King Melchior with his gift of incense; gallant young King Gaspard with his gift of treasure; black King Balthazar the Moor with his gift of myrrh. How reverently we would gaze on them, and how we would admire the brave pages who carried the trains of their long mantles, and the hump-backed camels whose heads towered high above Saint Mary and Saint Joseph and the ox and the ass.

Yes, there they were at last—the Kings!

Many and many a time in the after years have I gone a-walking on the Arles road at nightfall on the Eve of the Kings. It is the same—but not the same. The sun, over beyond the Rhône, is dipping toward the Cévennes; the leafless trees are red in the low sun-rays; across the fields stretch the black lines of cypress; even the old man, as long ago, is scratching in the hedge by the roadside for snails. And when darkness comes quickly, with the sun's setting, the owls hoot as of old.

But in the radiant glory of the sunset I no longer see the dazzle and the splendour of the Kings!

"Which way went they, the Kings?"

"Behind the mountains!"

VIII

In the morning of the day preceding Christmas a lurking, yet ill-repressed, excitement pervaded the Château and all its dependencies. In the case of the Vidame and Misè Fougueiroun the excitement did not even lurk: it blazed forth so openly that they were as a brace of comets—bustling violently through our universe and dragging into their erratic wakes, away from normal orbits, the whole planetary system of the household and all the haply intrusive stars.

With my morning coffee came the explanation of a quite impossible smell of frying dough-nuts which had puzzled me on the preceding day: a magnificent golden-brown *fougasso*, so perfect of its kind that any Provençal of that region—though he had come upon it in the sandy wastes of Sahara— would have known that its creator was Misè Fougueiroun. To compare the *fougasso* with our homely dough-nut does it injustice. It is a large flat open-work cake—a grating wrought in dough—an inch or so in thickness, either plain or sweetened or salted, fried delicately in the best olive-oil of Aix or Maussane. It is made throughout the winter, but its making at Christmas time is of obligation; and the custom obtains among the women—though less now than of old—of sending a *fougasso* as a Christmas gift to each of their intimates. As this custom had in it something more than a touch of vainglorious emulation, I well can understand why it has fallen into desuetude in the vicinity of Vièlmur—where Misè Fougueiroun's inspired kitchening throws all other cook-work hopelessly into the shade. As I ate the "horns" (as its fragments are called) of my *fougasso* that morning, dipping them in my coffee according to the prescribed custom, I was satisfied that it deserved its high place in the popular esteem.

When I joined the Vidame below stairs I found him under such stress of Christmas excitement that he actually forgot his usual morning suggestion—made always with an off-hand freshness, as though the matter were entirely new—that we should take a turn along the lines of the Roman Camp. He was fidgeting back and forth between the hall (our usual place of morning meeting) and the kitchen: torn by his conflicting desires to attend upon me, his guest, and to take his accustomed part in the friendly ceremony that was going on below. Presently he compromised the divergencies of the situation, though with some hesitation, by taking me down with him into Misè Fougueiroun's domain—where he became frankly cheerful when he found that I was well received.

Although the morning still was young, work on the estate had been ended for the day, and about the door of the kitchen more than a score of labourers were gathered: all with such gay looks as to show that something of a more than ordinarily joyous nature was in train. Among them I recognized the young fellow whom we had met with his wife carrying away the yule-log; and found that all of them were workmen upon the estate who—either being married or having homes within walking distance—were to be furloughed for the day. This was according to the Provençal custom that Christmas must be spent by one's own fire-side; and it also was according to Provençal custom that they were not suffered to go away with empty hands.

Misè Fougueiroun—a plump embodiment of Benevolence—stood beside a table on which was a great heap of her own *fougasso*, and big baskets filled with dried figs and almonds and celery, and a genial battalion of bottles standing guard over all. One by one the vassals were called up—there was a strong flavour of feudalism in it all—and to each, while the Vidame wished him a "*Bòni fèsto!*" the housekeeper gave his Christmas portion: a *fougasso*, a double-handful each of figs and almonds, a stalk of celery, and a bottle of *vin cue*[2]—the cordial that is used for the libation of the yule-log and for the solemn yule-cup; and each, as he received his portion, made his little speech of friendly thanks—in several cases most gracefully turned—and then was off in a hurry for his home. Most of them were dwellers in the immediate neighbourhood; but four or five had before them walks of more than twenty miles, with the same distance to cover in returning the next day. But great must be the difficulty or the distance that will keep a Provençal from his own people and his own hearth-stone at Christmas-tide!

In illustration of this home-seeking trait, I have from my friend Mistral the story that his own grandfather used to tell regularly every year when all the family was gathered about the yule-fire on Christmas Eve:

It was back in the Revolutionary times, and Mistral the grandfather—only he was not a grandfather then, but a mettlesome young soldier of two-and-twenty—was serving with the Army of the Pyrénées, down on the borders of Spain. December was well on, but the season was open—so open that he found one day a tree still bearing oranges. He filled a basket with the fruit and carried it to the Captain of his company. It was a gift for a king, down there in those hard times, and the Captain's eyes sparkled. "Ask what thou wilt, *mon brave*," he said, "and if I can give it to thee it shall be thine."

Quick as a flash the young fellow answered: "Before a cannon-ball cuts me in two, Commandant, I should like to go to Provence and help once more to lay the yule-log in my own home. Let me do that!"

Now that was a serious matter. But the Captain had given his word, and the word of a soldier of the Republic was better than the oath of a king. Therefore he sat down at his camp-table and wrote:

Army of the Eastern Pyrénées, December 12, 1793.

We, Perrin, Captain of Military Transport, give leave to the citizen François Mistral, a brave Republican soldier, twenty-two years old, five feet six inches high, chestnut hair and eyebrows, ordinary nose, mouth the same, round chin, medium forehead, oval face, to go back into his province, to go all over the Republic, and, if he wants to, to go to the devil!

"With an order like that in his pocket," said Mistral, "you can fancy how my grandfather put the leagues behind him; and how joyfully he reached

Maillane on the lovely Christmas Eve, and how there was danger of rib-cracking from the hugging that went on. But the next day it was another matter. News of his coming had flown about the town, and the Mayor sent for him.

"'In the name of the law, citizen,' the Mayor demanded, 'why hast thou left the army?'

"Now my grandfather was a bit of a wag, and so—with never a word about his famous pass—he answered: 'Well, you see I took a fancy to come and spend my Christmas here in Maillane.'

"At that the Mayor was in a towering passion. 'Very good, citizen,' he cried. 'Other people also may take fancies—and mine is that thou shalt explain this fancy of thine before the Military Tribunal at Tarascon. Off with him there!'

"And then away went my grandfather between a brace of gendarmes, who brought him in no time before the District Judge: a savage old fellow in a red cap, with a beard up to his eyes, who glared at him as he asked: 'Citizen, how is it that thou hast deserted thy flag?'

"Now my grandfather, who was a sensible man, knew that a joke might be carried too far; therefore he whipped out his pass and presented it, and so in a moment set everything right.

"'Good, very good, citizen!' said old Redcap. 'This is as it should be. Thy Captain says that thou art a brave soldier of the Republic, and that is the best that the best of us can be. With a pass like that in thy pocket thou canst snap thy fingers at all the mayors in Provence; and the devil himself had best be careful—shouldst thou go down that way, as thy pass permits thee—how he trifles with a brave soldier of France!'

"But my grandfather did not try the devil's temper," Mistral concluded. "He was satisfied to stay in his own dear home until the Day of the Kings was over, and then he went back to his command."

IX

The day dragged a little when we had finished in the kitchen with the giving of Christmas portions and the last of the farm-hands, calling back "*Bòni fèsto!*," had gone away. For the womenkind, of course, there was a world to do; and Misè Fougueiroun whisked us out of her dominions with a pretty plain statement that our company was less desirable than our room. But for the men there was only idle waiting until night should come.

As for the Vidame—who is a fiery fume of a little old gentleman, never happy unless in some way busily employed—this period of stagnation was so galling that in sheer pity I mounted him upon his hobby and set him to galloping away. 'Twas an easy matter, and the stimulant that I administered was rather dangerously strong: for I brought up the blackest beast in the whole herd of his abominations by asking him if there were not some colour of reason in the belief that Marius lay not at Vièlmur but at Glanum—now Saint-Remy-de-Provence—behind the lines of Roman wall which exist there to this day.

So far as relieving the strain of the situation was concerned, my expedient was a complete success; but the storm that I raised was like to have given the Vidame such an attack of bilious indigestion begotten of anger as would have spoiled the Great Supper for him; and as for myself, I was